JAWS™* 2
SHARKS:
**Everything That's Good
and Bad About Them**

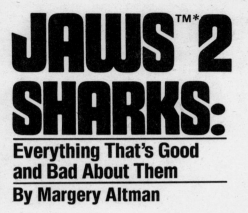

JAWS™*2 SHARKS:

Everything That's Good and Bad About Them

By Margery Altman

With pictures to color

Illustrated by Tony Tallarico

INKPOT BOOKS

GROSSET & DUNLAP
A FILMWAYS COMPANY
Publishers • New York

ACKNOWLEDGMENT

Many thanks to Sherm Milcowitz and the science students at the Simpson Waverly School in Hartford, Connecticut, who helped by asking questions on everything they wanted to know about sharks.

Library of Congress catalog card number: 78-58461
ISBN: 0-448-16336-5
*JAWS™ 2 is a trademark of and licensed by
Universal City Studios, Inc.
Published simultaneously in Canada.

Printed in the United States of America.

CONTENTS

Sharks predate the mighty dinosaur.

Were there sharks on earth during the age of dinosaurs?

Long before man appeared on earth, the shark was king of the seas. Rocks formed about 400 million years ago contain fossils of sharklike creatures. Fossils of true sharks have been found in rocks from the age of fishes, about 350 million years ago. Dinosaurs lived approximately 300 million years ago. It seems, therefore, that sharks predate the mighty dinosaur—and outlasted it.

Unlike dinosaur bones, shark skeletons are rarely found, because they are not true bones. The shark's skeletal system consists of cartilage, which is water soluble and disappears quickly.

With the passage of millions of years, many changes have occurred on earth. Different kinds of plants and animals, including dinosaurs, have appeared and disappeared. Sharks remain, and with very little change. Why these sea creatures have been able to survive for so many millions of years remains a mystery to scientists. Of course, they are perfectly adapted to the ocean, their habitat. And they are bold, aggressive animals, which can protect themselves against other sea animals, even those that are larger and more powerful.

Is a shark really a fish?

Scientific classification of living things places the shark in the animal kingdom. Man and shark share the same phylum—the chordata. This includes all vertebrates (animals with backbones), such as amphibians, reptiles, birds, fishes, and mammals. Sharks are in the class of chondrichthyes, or fish having cartilage instead of bones.

There are about 40,000 known species of fish. They are divided into three types—the cyclostomes, or eel-like creatures, having no jaws; the teleosts, fish having bony skeletons; and the selachians, which include sharks, rays, and skates, fish with cartilaginous skeletons.

Other structural differences between sharks and bony fish include the gills. Sharks have five to seven uncovered gill slits on each side of the head. Bony fish have one covered gill on each side of the head. Also, bony fish have air bladders, while sharks do not. This is an important difference since the air bladder keeps fish afloat.

These two types of fish also have different methods of reproduction. Bony fish lay eggs, which are fertilized in the water. The young hatch from the fertilized eggs. Sharks reproduce by copulation.

Yes! Sharks are fish, but they are fish of an unusual kind.

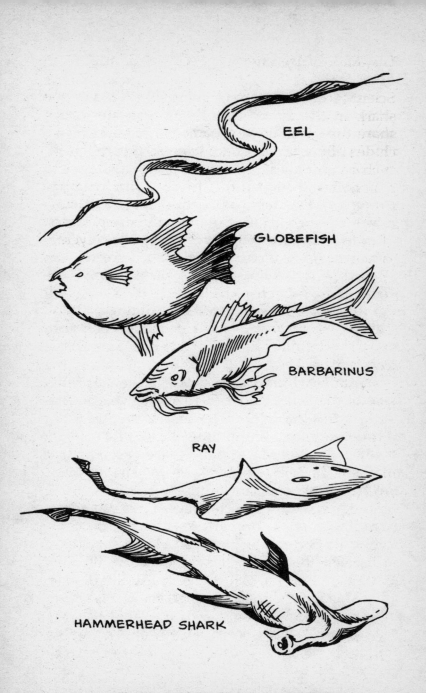

EEL

GLOBEFISH

BARBARINUS

RAY

HAMMERHEAD SHARK

Sharks are fish of an unusual kind.

How many different varieties of sharks are there?

The list of sharks extends well beyond the well-known tiger, hammerhead, great white, and whale. There are approximately 250 varieties of sharks in the seas.

One strange kind is the thresher shark, which is propelled by a tail that has tremendous driving power. Though it does not pose many dangers for man, it is extremely threatening to other sea creatures. A sea bird, for instance, can easily be swatted by the shark's tail.

The goblin shark, a deep-water dweller, is 14 feet long, has long sharp teeth, and a paddle-shaped nose. Scientists think its features suggest what sharks may have looked like 60 million years ago.

Lemon sharks are deep yellow in color. Some have been trained to swim to submarine targets and return for a reward of food.

Though sharks are among the easiest fish to identify, the different varieties are difficult to distinguish. Their external features or shapes usually help classify them, and their names often describe physical characteristics. Here are some examples: the frilled shark has many frilly gills around its body. The carpet shark has a coating on its skin that looks like a sea bed. The silky shark has smooth skin. The spiny shark has spiny skin. And the seven-gilled shark has seven gills.

Two sharks have been named after common household pets, the cat shark and the dog shark. Can you guess why?

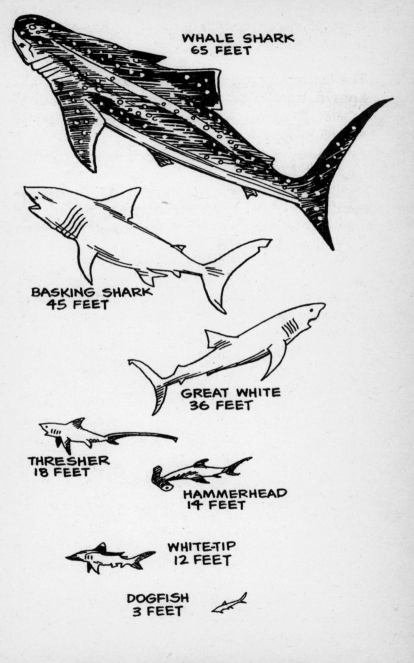

WHALE SHARK
65 FEET

BASKING SHARK
45 FEET

GREAT WHITE
36 FEET

THRESHER
18 FEET

HAMMERHEAD
14 FEET

WHITE-TIP
12 FEET

DOGFISH
3 FEET

There are about 250 varieties of sharks.

Can sharks live in fresh water as well as salt water?

The shark is best suited for life in salt water because of its blood chemistry and gill system.

But sharks have traveled to fresh water and adapted to life there. The bull shark, which has a record of attacking humans, will sometimes travel to fresh-water rivers to do so.

One possible explanation for the upstream movement of sharks may be that they are searching for food. Hungry sharks have been known to travel for hundreds of miles. Sometimes they become locked in inlets and are forced to adapt in order to survive.

Fresh-water sharks are found mainly within the latitudes of 30 degrees North and 30 degrees South. They are virtually unknown in the fresh waters of Europe or northern Asia. Only in tropical regions can they find an environment where the temperature is suitable and the fluctuations minimal.

Two varieties of fresh-water sharks are the Ganges shark, which lives exclusively in fresh water, and the Zambezi shark, which lives in Africa and has a reputation for ferocity and unprovoked attacks. The lemon shark is typically an Atlantic Ocean dweller, but has been found in the rivers of South America.

The shark is best suited for life in salt water.

Do sharks hatch from eggs?

Most female sharks give birth to live babies. The mother keeps her eggs inside her body, where the male fertilizes them by implanting sperm. The young are born alive after a gestation period of eight to nine months. Once born, baby sharks receive no attention from either their mothers or fathers. The fathers may even eat the baby sharks.

Litters are sometimes small, containing only two to four babies, but they can be large. The tiger shark, for instance, can bear up to eighty-two babies in one litter.

The baby shark's size at birth is proportionate to the size of its mother. Great white shark babies average 3 to 5 feet. Lemon shark babies measure about 2 feet in length, while their mother is between 7 and 10 feet long.

Young sharks are well equipped for a free life in the ocean. They have a full set of teeth. Their skin is covered with rough denticles, and their fins are workable. The survival rate of newborn sharks is higher than that of many other kinds of fish, because they are ready to defend themselves at birth. In fact, very young sharks have been known to attack man.

Sharks give birth to live babies.

Which is the largest of all sharks?

The great whale shark is considered by some scientists to be even bigger than the whale itself. Some prehistoric fish may have been larger than the 45 foot whale sharks known today, but it is hard to imagine such a fish. Fishermen tell of sighting 60 foot whale sharks, but few have ever been caught. One landed in India drew over 100,000 spectators in a very short time.

Whale sharks never seem to bother man. But they sometimes give us a scare because of their immense size. The raft Kon Tiki ran into one at sea. The impact was so strong that it was like hitting a train. Luckily, both the animal and the raft survived the crash. The great whale shark doesn't seem to be interested in man.

For food it seeks schools of fish, squid, and crustacians. The giant jaws ingest all kinds of fish. The smaller fish are strained into the stomach. At feeding time the whale shark, in a vertical position, simply lets the small fish wash into its mouth and gill strainers.

A myth about the whale shark feeding on tuna is not true. The reason the largest shark follows this fish is that small fish are usually found around tuna, thus providing whale shark with a good meal.

The great whale shark is found mostly in tropical areas, though some have been found as far south as Brazil and as far north as Long Island, New York. The Gulf of California, the Red Sea, and the Indian Ocean are also known habitats for these fish.

The great whale shark is the largest in the seas.

What Color is a Shark?

Most fish are attractive to look at because of their graceful forms and their beautiful colors. Sharks are an exception!

They are basically different shadings of one color. Their bellies are light, while their backs are dark. Names of sharks often derive from their main body color—great white, great blue, Australian grey nurse shark, black-tip, white-tip, lemon shark, and so on. Sometimes they are named for their color patterns—marbled tiger, brown smoothhound, black spotted, frilled, zebra, spotted dog, carpet, or spiny shark.

The most colorful sharks are members of the Orectolobidae family. This group includes carpet sharks, nurse sharks, and wobbegongs. They are relatively small in size and are reef-dwellers. Divers are attracted to them because they are beautiful, but they can be dangerous.

The sharks' shading, like that of other animals, is said to be nature's way of protecting them. Certain species have the ability to become lighter or darker in coloration to blend with the surrounding area of water. The ability to change color comes from the shark's skin pigmentation. The color cells react via the nervous system. Experiments continue in an effort to learn more about the shark's use of coloration as a means of protecting itself.

They are basically different shades of one color.

Do Sharks have keen eyesight?

Studies of shark vision have been particularly interesting. They seem to be able to react to environmental changes quickly, but see only feebly, at best. The eyes play a small role in its reactions. What the shark does sense is a change in light or color, or the presence of another being in its vicinity.

Experiments have shown that sharks can adjust to sudden darkness within only ten seconds. This is half the human reaction-time of twenty seconds. The reason for the quick reaction is that the animal's pupil expands more rapidly than the human pupil when adjusting to changes in light. They can also see in deep waters and dim caves, where humans cannot.

Sharks have rigid lenses in their eyes. In most cases these lenses are controlled by a muscle, which moves them toward or away from the light-sensitive retina.

One indication that the shark's eyes are poor is that when the animal's sense of smell is blocked in tests the shark seems helpless and at times even injures itself.

Sharks have poor eyesight.

Does the shark have a good sense of smell?

The sense of smell is one way that the shark identifies its prey. It has an excellent sense of smell, and the ability to detect the presence of food or blood up to a quarter of a mile away. The extent to which a shark can rely on its sense of smell depends on how diluted the odorous substance is in the water.

Anatomically speaking, the smell mechanism of the shark is similar to that of man. The pits on its snout are similar to the nostrils of a person's nose. Mucus inside picks up the smells of the sea. As the current washes over the shark, the smell-oriented brain tells it what is going on around it.

Experiments have demonstrated that the sense of smell can lead a shark to food many miles away. But if its nose is blocked, it can swim right past food and not know it is there. A shark traveling in a zig-zag pattern is most likely "following its nose."

Its sense of smell helps the shark identify its prey.

Can sharks hear?

Sharks' ability to hear and to distinguish a variety of low-frequency sounds helps these animals track moving prey. Fish continually create echoes and sonic impulses under water, and sea creatures use these signals to navigate.

The shark has no external ears. It relies on its lateral nerves to feel water vibrations on its body. It can distinguish sonic waves up to 640 cycles per second and hear sounds thousands of yards away. The curious fish follows sound waves to the source of noise. When it is within 50 feet of its prey, the shark's eyes become the primary sensory organ used.

Scientists have discovered that there are specific sounds that sharks dislike. Studies are under way to gather information about these sounds in order to use them as anti-shark protection. Swimmers could, perhaps, carry noise-making devices that would keep sharks away.

Sharks can distinguish a variety of low-frequency sounds.

Do sharks ever lose their teeth?

Because they're put to such strenuous use, shark teeth are replaced often. Young sharks lose their teeth very easily. Scientists suspect that an adult gets a whole new set of teeth annually.

Shark teeth are not implanted in sockets like mammals' teeth, but are anchored to the jaw. The teeth grow in rows. As soon as one set of teeth falls out or becomes worn out from hard use, the row directly underneath becomes functional.

The strength of a particular type of shark's teeth is proportionate to the power of its jaws. One shark tooth alone can apply a force equal to 3 metric tons per square centimeter. The parts of the jaws work together. The teeth in the lower jaw hold the prey while the teeth in the upper jaw tear it apart. Shark jaws can shred 25 to 30 pounds of matter in one bite.

Scientists have used sharks' teeth to help classify these animals. The great white has triangle-shaped teeth. The tiger has broader based, but extremely sharp, teeth. Long tapered teeth are found in sand and mako sharks.

Because sharks replace their teeth so frequently, lucky beachcombers have found souvenir teeth along the shore.

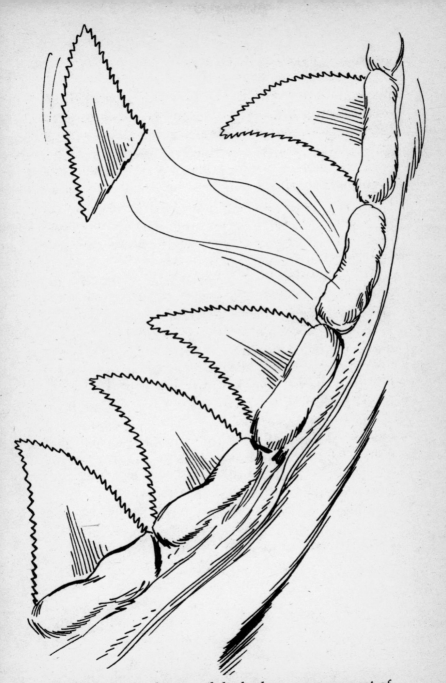

Scientists suspect that an adult shark grows a new set of
teeth annually.

What does a shark eat?

The simple answer is: ALMOST ANYTHING! Most sharks will eat anything—living or nonliving. Some even eat other sharks. For this reason, this is one species of fish that does not travel in schools.

Although a hungry shark is not choosy about its food, it does have preferences. For example, the nurse eats crustaceans; the bull hunts crabmeat or pieces of other sharks; the tiger likes crab, mackerel, turtle, and even hammerhead-shark meat; the hammerhead prefers shad and crustaceans; the mako seeks bluefish. That is why most sea creatures fear sharks.

Anything a shark has consumed may be found whole in its stomach. What is edible doesn't always matter. Such garbage as tin cans and pieces of wood have been found in their digestive tracts. Sailors who have fished for sharks tell of seeing such parts of boats as wooden pegs, rope, and metal hardware inside their catches.

There is a story about a pirateer who threw the evidence of his crime overboard at sea. Unfortunately for him a shark ate the documents. A short time later, the fish was caught by some fishermen several miles away. During the pirateer's trial, the incriminating information was produced and he was convicted.

A shark eats only 4 to 10 percent of its own body weight each week. Thus there are times when it does not eat. Young sharks, like children, need lots of food to help them grow and develop. But adults survive on less food.

Sharks' feeding habits are not well under-

Sharks eat almost anything.

stood. Fishermen have seen them approach food and then retreat in disinterest—only to return shortly to devour the same food. At other times they grab anything in sight. Hunger does not seem to be the prime motivation for the shark's eating behavior, which is still being studied by scientists.

Do sharks ever sleep?

It is difficult for us as mammals to imagine life without sleep. But sharks cannot sleep! Researchers explain that because they lack air bladders, which keep most other fish afloat, sharks must move their pectoral fins constantly to counteract their weight. The moment this movement stops, they sink.

Nevertheless, they do have periods of apparent tranquility. This state seems to be caused by the condition of the water and other living things in it. The cave areas in which sharks are often-found have contained large amounts of carbon-dioxide gas, which seem to dull the fishes' senses. Other chemical properties of the water also change. The amount of salt and the number of parasitic animals living off sharks' bodies are reduced. Caves seem to act as cleansing stations, removing wastes from their systems.

Sharks can't sleep.

Are most sharks lazy?

The basking shark is often considered lazy because it just floats on the surface of the water. Although it is one of the two largest sharks (the other is the great whale), its diet consists mainly of plankton (small microscopic animals). As the ocean currents wash up against the fish's body, plankton filters in through its large gill system.

Sportfishermen say this 35 to 40 foot fish has tremendous strength and puts up a good fight when it is caught. On the other hand commercial fishermen consider it a nuisance, since it often gets caught in a fishing net or scares off a potential catch.

Although it is not typically a man-eater, the basking shark is considered dangerous because of its great size and power.

Which are the fiercest sharks?

Man fears all sharks because of their power, unpredictability and capacity to eat almost anything that moves. A few types of sharks have been singled out as the most dangerous of all.

The tiger shark is one of the most notorious man-eaters of the sea. It seems to eat anything that moves. Human bodies as well as tin cans have been found in its stomach. Its jaws are among the most powerful in the world, and it has been known to gobble its prey in one bite. The teeth are so sharp and pointed that they can catch victims of any size. Few escape its grasp.

The basking shark is considered lazy.

Most of what the tiger eats is swallowed whole or in large pieces. At times it eats ferociously, while at other times it eats nothing at all.

The tiger shark is rare in northern waters and more common in the tropics. Often this fish will enter shallow water in search of a meal. This is when it is most dangerous to man.

Though tiger sharks are not prominent in most fishing waters, fishermen considered them valuable catches. Their livers are rich in vitamin-A, and the hides make fine leather products.

The bull kills more people than any other type of shark. It inhabits shallow waters near populated centers. This fish can also adapt to life in fresh waters. Some have been found in the inland lakes of Nicaragua. The bull is the most common shark of Florida and is found there all year long. It has also been sighted in as little as 3 to 4 feet of water. One characteristic is a black-tipped fin sticking out of the water. Their attack is so vicious that they have been known to continue their pursuit of victims right onto the shore.

The mako shark is popular among sport fishermen. It is the fastest swimmer and thus a real challenge to catch. The mako can move fast through the water because of its streamlined body.

Unlike other popular sportfish, such as the mackeral shark, which inhabits cold water, the mako shark is found in warm water. Both these sport sharks inhabit deep waters and are known to attack fishermen and their boats. Not typically man-eaters, their favorite food is swift-moving swordfish.

The tiger shark is one of the most notorious man-eaters of the sea.

The mako shark is most commonly caught off the coasts of Australia and New Zealand. It was named after a New Zealand Indian called Mooris. This Indian hunter went out in canoes, seeking the large center tooth of that shark. Catching such a fast-moving animal in only a canoe seemed impossible, but this hunter was determined to accomplish that feat as well as the trick of extracting the center tooth of the fierce fish.

Which are the most dangerous sharks?

The meanest and most dangerous shark of the sea is the great white, though it is not quite as large as the huge basking or whale sharks since it grows only to 35 or 40 feet. A warm-blooded creature, its higher body temperature makes its muscles stronger than those of most other varieties of sharks.

Considered a killer, the great white is unchallenged anywhere in the ocean. It has been known to eat anything in sight, and at times swallows its prey in one bite. Scientists discovered a whole sea lion in one great white, and a whole horse in another.

This fish is most often found in the tropics, but a few have been caught in northern regions during the warmer months. It requires a great deal of ocean space, travels alone, and is hard to spot. The great white can be identified by its huge size, rigid body, large mouth, large triangular teeth, large pectoral fin, and fast movement.

The most dangerous shark is the great white.

Sportfishermen say that catching a great white is like towing a submarine.

The hammerhead shark, also extremely dangerous, has a T-bar-shaped head, and its eyes can be as far apart as 36 inches. The strange head shape helps keep the fish stable. Highly developed sensory cells for smell and sight make the hammerhead one of the most skillful of the sea killers.

This deep-water dweller travels from the tropics to the northern waters during the summer and attacks anything that moves. Strong and ferocious, it is increasingly threatening to man because it is one of the most plentiful sharks in the sea.

Why do sharks attack humans?

The factors that influence the actions of a shark are usually beyond the control of the swimmer. But in some cases humans have caused serious attacks.

The presence of a recently speared fish will cause a curious shark to attack. Divers are advised to carry containers in which to conceal their catches. Impeding a shark's movements might also cause it to attack. Reports have been made about divers who have attempted to spear or catch them by the tail. In such cases seemingly docile sharks have turned against divers and their boats.

The zookeeper's advice, "Don't feed the bears" applies to even the most harmless sharks.

Sometimes humans provoke serious attacks.

They may appreciate your kind gift of food but are not likely to understand where the food ends and the hand begins. The excitement of a single shark increases if it is part of a school of feeding sharks. It may become affected by a "feeding frenzy," in which several of the fish simultaneously attack the same bait—be it fish, human, or anything else, including a tin can or wooden box. A shark indiscriminately attacks and consumes it.

In some cases, injuries are caused by bumps rather than by bites. Some sharks run into objects that attract them, perhaps as a way of testing whether or not the objects are edible. Usually it does not bite the victim right away. Some researchers think a shark's bump is meant to be a friendly gesture.

What can swimmers do to avoid a shark's attack?

Swimming in the sea or ocean is fun, but it can be dangerous. Shark behavior is unpredictable, and relatively little is known about their habits or patterns.

Experts advise swimmers to take the following precautions:
- Always swim with a companion.
- Do not stay in the water with a bleeding wound. Blood attracts them.
- Avoid swimming in murky waters or at night, when underwater visibility is poor.
- If you see a shark, do not provoke it, hang onto its tail, or attempt to ride it.

Adopt a sensible attitude.

- Get out of the water as quickly as possible if you see a shark nearby.
- Try to remain calm. If you cannot get out of the water in time, stay still and keep the animal in sight at all times.

The most important advice given by authorities on sharks is to adopt a sensible attitude toward them. Statistics prove that the likelihood of being attacked is smaller than that of being struck by lightning. Swimmers should continue to enjoy the sport while looking out for their own safety.

Does the shark have any friends?

Despite its reputation as a monster that eats anything, the shark does have a "friendly" relationship with a few sea creatures. "Friendly" in this case, however, might mean only tolerable.

Pilot fish never seem to be attacked by sharks. The two have a symbiotic relationship—they help each other. Scouting for schools of fish for food, the shark follows the very small pilot fish, which also benefit, as they feed on what the shark has left.

Sailors' legends tell about pilot fish that hunt for feeding areas and then act as guides to bring sharks to the site.

Pilot fish have never been found in a shark's stomach. One possible explanation is that they do not taste good to a shark. Or perhaps by not eating them, the larger animals reward them for their help.

Pilot fish are never attacked by sharks.

Another sea creature, the remora fish has a different kind of friendship with the shark. This fish is interested in a "free ride." It attaches itself to any large fish and travels with it in the water. Although it has been known to cling to turtles, whales, swordfish, and other sea creatures, it finds its best meals when it is with a shark. As the shark chops up its food, the remora gobbles up the crumbs.

Sharks have been known to eat remoras, but rarely. In an effort to get a free meal, a remora attaches itself to the inside of the larger animal's jaws. As the shark digests its meal, it also eats the remora.

Primitive fishermen used to catch many fish, including sharks, using the remoras as bait. A remora with the hook would attach itself to the fish's back, and the fisherman would have a catch.

In the cases of both the pilot fish and the remora fish, the seemingly greedy and unfriendly shark has tolerated other sea creatures.

Does the shark have enemies?

Even a big and powerful fish like the shark has enemies. Frequently smaller, less powerful creatures challenge it and win.

One great foe is not large at all. It is called the Moses sole. A shark will not swim in any area inhabited by this fish. Although the Moses sole is often cooked and eatenly safely, it contains a highly poisonous milky substance, which, if ingested, can paralyze any living thing.

Old or sick sharks are often attacked and devoured by other sharks.

Although the killer whale's food usually consists of dolphins, seals, and other smaller marine animals, this giant sea creature has been known to eat sharks. Sperm whales also occasionally attack them with their powerful and sharp teeth.

Still another enemy is the swordfish. Its sword, made of razor-sharp bone, is capable of fatally injuring a shark.

A major foe is man. Humans attack them for many reasons. Fear and hatred of these sea creatures has turned many sportfishermen into "monster hunters." Catching and killing them gives the fisherman a great sense of triumph. But sharks are also valued for the products derived from them, including liver oil, leather, teeth, and meat.

Thus sharks, though very able to defend themselves, are not entirely safe from other predators.

Even a big powerful fish like the shark has enemies.

Are sharkskins valuable?

Sharkskins were first used by Greek artisans. The craftsmen rubbed the leather against hard wood to smooth and polish it.

Later, travelers returning from the Orient brought hand-crafted cases covered with shark leather back to Europe. This rare and beautiful leather was also used by artists in Holland and France. Portrait frames, leather cases, and watchbands were among the items made of sharkskin.

Recently, a Syracuse, New York, shoe manufacturer began promoting shark-leather shoes. Sixty dollars a pair is not considered a high price for men's shoes made of this material. It does not scuff and it is long-lasting. High-priced suitcases, wallets, attachés, and belts made of sharkskin also appear in today's stores. Because of its toughness, shark leather is ideal for cowboy boots, ski boots, and the tips of children's shoes.

Fishermen are paid a good price for the animal's hide. The price is based on the it's size, condition, and the type of shark it comes from. The length is most important, since the piece of leather must be large enough to make a product. Tiger sharks are considered valuable catches. The fisherman who catches one can sell it for anywhere from $2 to $14, depending upon its size.

The sharkskin is one *good* thing about a shark.

Sharkskins are used for shoes, belts, and other leather products.

Is shark meat good to eat?

Shark-fin soup was an ancient Chinese delicacy. Serving this sacred dish was said to honor one's guests. Failing to serve the soup signaled the host's disfavor with the guests.

More recently, the United Nations has sponsored food research and found some ways to use shark meat for food. One popular method is to grind the meat into a fine particles to produce fish flour. It is like the wheat flour we use to make breads, but it is more nutritious. Fish flour contains 85 percent animal protein and is one of the most highly concentrated forms of protein used by man. This product is relatively low in cost and can be used to make a variety of food items, from bread to spaghetti.

Japanese natives consume shark meat in great quantities. It is sold there fresh, canned, and smoked. Smoked shark meat is also exported. Lower grades of the meat are served in the form of fish cakes. Japanese style soya sauce is often used to flavor it.

Shark meat has not been readily available in the United States until recently. In a Houston, Texas, supermarket a salesperson offered shoppers free breaded and fried shark meat. Some people were reluctant to try the samples, but many who did enjoyed the delicacy.

The taste of shark meat has been compared to that of a Gulf fish such as redfish. Shark meat can be prepared much like any other fish—baked, fried, broiled, grilled, smoked, and even served with a sauce. Perhaps it will one day become a seafood delicacy for Americans.

Shark-fin soup was an ancient Chinese delicacy.

What good is shark liver?

The shark's liver is huge—sometimes weighing one sixth as much as the entire animal. It helps the shark stay afloat because this fish lacks an air bladder, the floating mechanism of most other fish. The liver also stores food, and since its size varies with the size of the fish, it helps determine how regularly the fish will eat.

Shark fishermen prize the liver because it is so rich in oil, one fish providing as much as 60 to 70 gallons. In fishing towns like Monteray, California, it is considered big business.

Shark-liver oil contains more vitamin A than cod-liver oil and is used in many industries, including the production of vitamins, margarine, drugs, soap, cosmetics, paints, and lubricants. It is also useful in leather tanning and in cancer and heart-disease research.

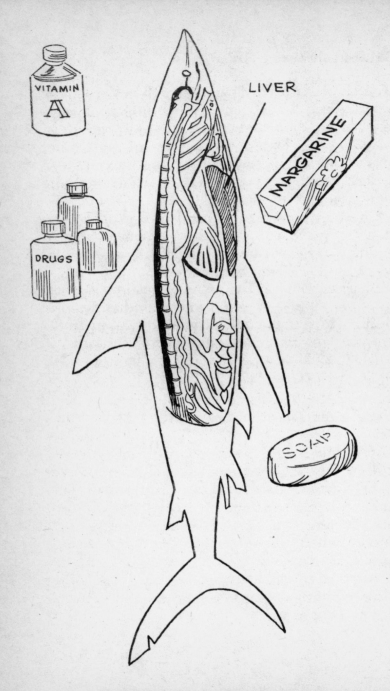

Shark-liver oil is used in many industries.

How can sharks help man?

Medical researchers report that sharks have been useful to them in their search for cures for cancer and other puzzling diseases. Some medical studies in which shark matter has been used are kidney physiology and body metabolism. Shark urine has also aided in experiments on fat-soluble drugs.

Some scientists believe sharks may hold the secret to the development of antibodies, which may help men become immune to some diseases. One facility at which such research is taking place is the Lerner Marine Laboratory, located on Bimini, an island off the Florida coast. There, sharks are captured in nets, tagged, and placed in pools of anesthetizing fluid.

After a shark becomes calm it is taken to a testing room, where blood and body-fluid samples are extracted. The fish is then returned to a pen, where it remains until needed for another sample.

Meanwhile, the specimens are studied carefully in the lab. Past experiments have shown that sharks have an unusual and powerful immune system, which helps them fight off disease. Bacteria, viruses, and cancer cells are all affected when combined with shark blood. Because cancer cells are killed when mixed with shark-blood serum, scientists hope a study of the animal's immune system will eventually lead to a cure for cancer.

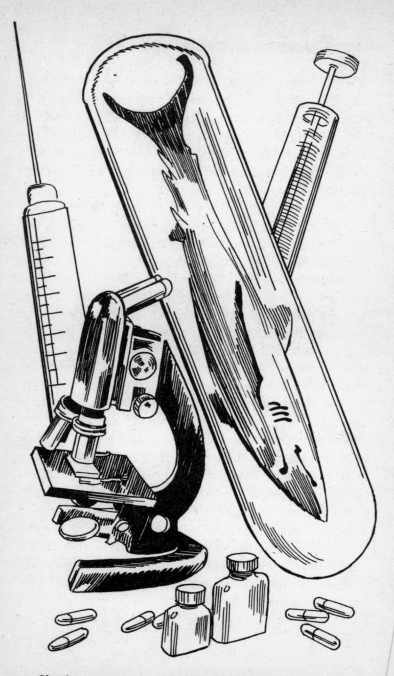

Sharks are useful in the search for cures for disease.

Which sharks are considered game fish?

The shark is often sought after as a sportfish, which game fishermen seldom kill unless they are entered in a competition. They view sharks as among the best large catches, and claim that use of a light tackle to catch one can be great fun. Some enjoy seeing the mako shark, for instance, doing its acrobatic tricks. Black-tips jump as high as 15 feet in the air and spin at the same time.

The International Game Fish Association has identified seven kinds of sharks as game fish. Here are some interesting records. The hammerhead has been found from Cape Cod southward in the Atlantic. The largest one caught weighed 703 pounds. Most great blues that have been caught have been 5 to 7 feet long and weighed just under 200 pounds. They are found mostly along the Atlantic coast, in the Caribbean, and in the Pacific.

The largest thresher ever caught weighed 739 pounds and was caught in New Zealand waters. Although the thresher has not been known to attack man, its tail is considered dangerous.

The great white, best known as the "man-eater," has often been found in the Atlantic. A great white weighing 2,664 pounds was the largest fish ever to be caught on a rod and reel. The shortfin mako has been considered the "sportiest" shark, because it is fast and beautiful. It has been known to jump into boats. The largest one was caught in New Zealand and weighed 1,061 pounds. The tiger is found in warm tropical waters. The largest catch, weighing 1,780 pounds

Many varieties of sharks are sought after as game fish.

and measuring 13 feet in length, was off the coast of South Carolina. Although the porbeagle is related to the great white, none has been known to attack man. The world record catch of this variety was a 430 pound fish taken in England.

SHARK QUIZ

1   When did sharks first inhabit the earth?
2   How large is a whale shark?
3   Which waters do tiger sharks usually
    inhabit?
4   Are there any fish that sharks do not eat?
5   How much protein does fish flour contain?
6   What was the weight of the largest great
    white shark ever caught?
7   How do scientists classify different varieties
    of sharks?
8   Colorful sharks are members of which
    family?
9   Is the shark smell mechanism very different
    from that of man?
10 If a shark loses a tooth, is it ever replaced?
11 How much does a shark eat weekly?
12 How far apart are a hammerhead shark's
    eyes?
13 Name two kinds of sharks that are named
    after household pets?
14 Do scientists really understand shark
    behavior?
15 How did the ancient Greeks use sharkskin?
16 What waters does the great blue shark
    usually inhabit?
17 Are sharks used in medical research?

41 Why is the Moses sole so dangerous to sharks?
42 Which part of the shark is often taken as a souvenir?
43 How can shark hide be used?
44 If you were game fishing for a great white shark, where do you look for it?
45 Can sharks see in deep waters?
46 Do sharks have the ability to change color?
47 Are there any African fresh-water sharks?
48 How many gill slits do sharks have?
49 Which shark inhabits the Indian Ocean?
50 How many species of sharks are there?